NEVER FLIRT WITH PUPPY KILLERS

NEVER FLIRT WITH PUPPY KILLERS

AND OTHER BETTER BOOK TITLES

DAN WILBUR

Andrews McMeel Publishing®

a division of Andrews McMeel Universal

Introduction

If brevity is the soul of wit, then this is the wittiest book ever written because there are barely any words in it. Your definition of wit, however, will also have to include using the word "handjob" to sum up the modernist classic *Ulysses* by James Joyce. If you're not into reading the word "handjob" in print and laughing, this probably isn't the book for you. (I'd also stay away from James Joyce altogether. His books have a lot to do with jerking off, both literally and figuratively.)

If you're a "big reader" or know someone who is, then this is the book you've been waiting for your whole life. I promise you: No one else in comedy is making jokes about *Gilgamesh* or *Madame Bovary.* Whether you majored in English and plan to do nothing with your degree, or you're currently a librarian wondering if you should let a child check out this book, take a look inside. You won't be disappointed.

Never Flirt with Puppy Killers is based on the wildly popular Tumblr betterbooktitles.com, and includes the favorite fake covers from the site. From children's literature like *The Very Hungry Caterpillar* getting the retitle *Eat Until You Feel Pretty,* to an American classic like *The Great Gatsby* getting switched to *Drink Responsibly,* there's something in here for every reader. If you can't find one you like, then you probably don't read enough. The good news is that you'll soon know what all those huge tomes you skipped in high school and college are about just by skimming this book.

Finally, you can judge a book by its cover.

Contents

"Classics"
The Books You've Lied About Reading

Actual Classics
Greek, Latin, and Epics in Other Languages People
Don't Even Pretend to Have Read

Children's
Books that Say the Most with the Fewest Number of Words, i.e.,
"The Best Books"

Young Adult
Books Written for Children that Adults Still Read

Nonfiction & Reference
Those Books that Were Around Before Google

Theater
Books that Are Objectively Better if Paid Actors Read Them to You

Holiday
Mostly Picture Books that Your Faith Requires You to at
Least Think About Once a Year

Summer Reading
Books You Read the Day Before the Test at School

Contemporary Fiction
Those Books People Talk About at Parties that
"You've Definitely Heard of"
but Never Bothered to Pick Up

"Classics"

The Books You've
Lied About Reading

F. Scott Fitzgerald, *The Great Gatsby*

Getting Fondled at the County Fair

A New Translation by LYDIA DAVIS

Gustave Flaubert

Gustave Flaubert, *Madame Bovary*

Oscar Wilde, *The Picture of Dorian Gray*

The Timeless Classic of Growing Up and the Human Dignity That Unites Us All

MY DAD IS COOLER THAN YOUR DAD

Harper Lee

Harper Lee, *To Kill a Mockingbird*
Submitted by Elihu Dietz

ONE LONG SENTENCE ABOUT HANDJOBS

BY

JAMES JOYCE

James Joyce, *Ulysses*

PENGUIN CLASSICS

MARK TWAIN

One of My Best Friends Is Black

Mark Twain, *The Adventures of Huckleberry Finn*
Submitted by David and Michael Molina

13

Sir Arthur Conan Doyle, *The Adventures of Sherlock Holmes*

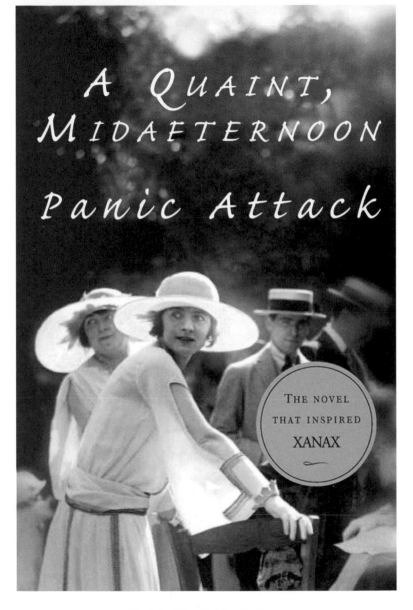

A Quaint, Midafternoon Panic Attack

THE NOVEL THAT INSPIRED XANAX

Virginia Woolf, *Mrs. Dalloway*

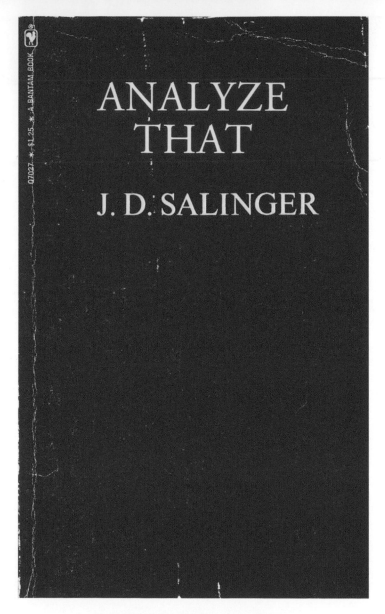

ANALYZE
THAT

J. D. SALINGER

J. D. Salinger, *The Catcher in the Rye*

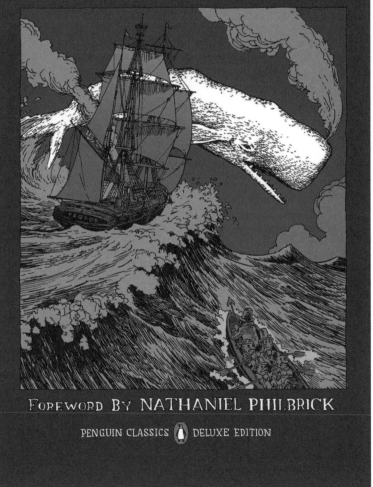

Herman Melville, *Moby Dick*

WORDSWORTH CLASSICS

EMOTIONS ARE FOR POOR PEOPLE

EDITH WHARTON

Edith Wharton, *The Age of Innocence*
Submitted by Michelle Legro

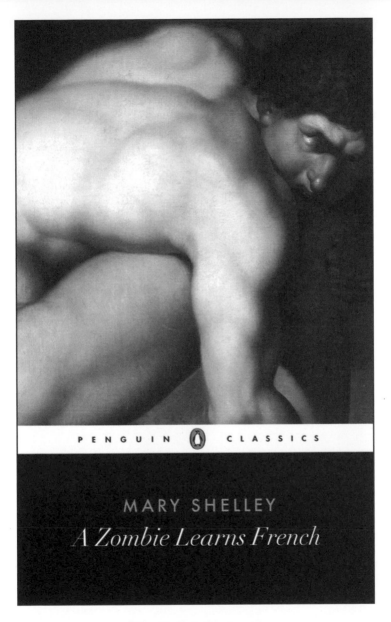

PENGUIN CLASSICS

MARY SHELLEY

A Zombie Learns French

Mary Shelley, *Frankenstein*

THE GOOD ONES ARE ALWAYS TAKEN

ALWAYS TAKEN

(BY CRAZY CHICKS)

Charlotte Brontë, *Jane Eyre*

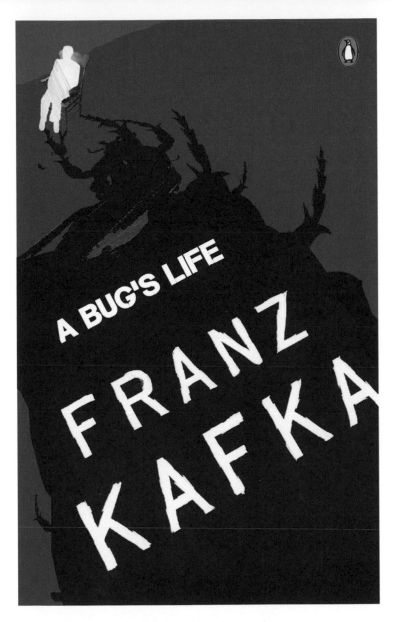

Franz Kafka, *The Metamorphosis*

Actual Classics

Greek, Latin, and Epics
in Other Languages
People Don't Even
Pretend to Have Read

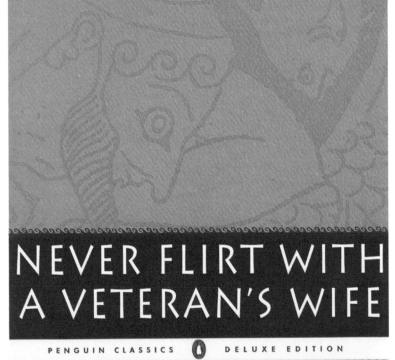

HOMER

**NEVER FLIRT WITH
A VETERAN'S WIFE**

PENGUIN CLASSICS ✦ DELUXE EDITION

TRANSLATED BY
ROBERT FAGLES

INTRODUCTION AND NOTES BY BERNARD KNOX

One of the ten "Best Books of 1996"—TIME

Homer, *Odyssey*

HOMER

AN ANGRY GUY GETS ANGRIER THEN CHILLS

PENGUIN CLASSICS ● DELUXE EDITION

TRANSLATED BY
ROBERT FAGLES
INTRODUCTION AND NOTES BY BERNARD KNOX
Winner of an Academy of American Poets Landon Translation Award

Homer, *Illiad*

PENGUIN CLASSICS

APOLLONIUS OF RHODES

*An Entire Frat Sets Sail to Steal
the World's Fanciest Coat*

Apollonius of Rhodes, *Argonautica*

PENGUIN CLASSICS

THE EPIC FOR PEOPLE WHO DON'T LIKE EPIC-LENGTH EPICS

Epic of Gilgamesh

PENGUIN CLASSICS

DANTE

Satan Is a Huge Asshole . . . Literally!

Dante, *Divine Comedy: Volume 1: Inferno*

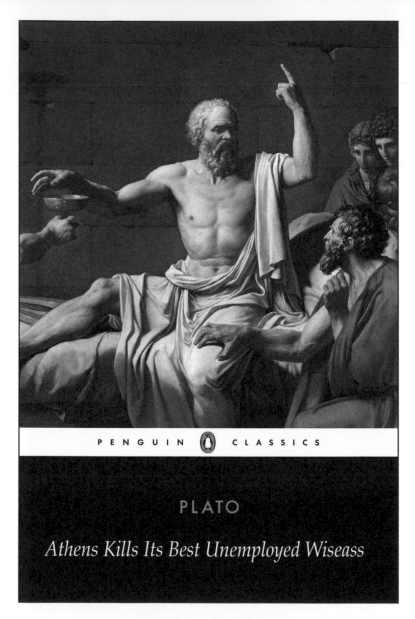

PENGUIN CLASSICS

PLATO

Athens Kills Its Best Unemployed Wiseass

Plato, *The Last Days of Socrates*

DADDY ISSUES
AND A
BAD BREAKUP
FOUND ROME

VIRGIL

TRANSLATED BY

ROBERT FAGLES

INTRODUCTION BY BERNARD KNOX

PENGUIN CLASSICS ✦ DELUXE EDITION

Virgil, *Aeneid*

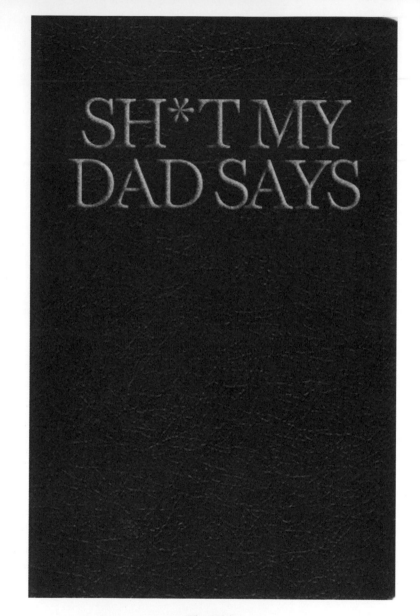

The Bible
Submitted by Django Haskins

Children's

Books that Say the
Most with the Fewest
Number of Words,
i.e., "The Best Books"

Call
Your
Mom
by
Shel
Silverstein

Shel Silverstein, *The Giving Tree*

The Last Story Grandpa Told Us Before We Sent Him to the Home

Written by Judi Barrett
and Drawn by Ron Barrett

Judi Barrett and Ron Barrett, *Cloudy with a Chance of Meatballs*

Dr. Seuss, *Oh, The Places You'll Go!*
Submitted by Tyler Snodgrass

EAT UNTIL YOU FEEL PRETTY
by Eric Carle

Eric Carle, *The Very Hungry Caterpillar*

Roald Dahl

It's OK If Giant Fruit Kills Your Aunts so long as They Were Bitches

With full-colour illustrations by Quentin Blake

Roald Dahl, *James and the Giant Peach*

Cheer Up. This Is How You'll Feel *Every* Day as an Adult.

JUDITH VIORST

Illustrated by RAY CRUZ

Judith Viorst and Ray Cruz, *Alexander and the Terrible, Horrible, No Good, Very Bad Day*

IF SOMEONE LIES TO YOU, MURDER HIM AND LIE ABOUT MURDERING HIM

JON KLASSEN

Jon Klassen, *I Want My Hat Back*

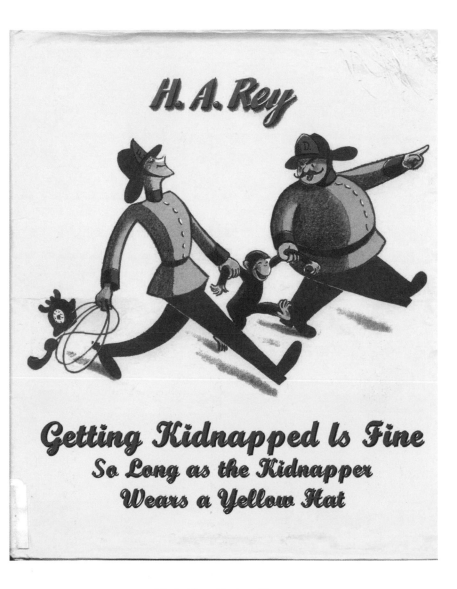

Getting Kidnapped Is Fine
So Long as the Kidnapper
Wears a Yellow Hat

H. A. Rey, *Curious George*

LEWIS CARROLL

INSIDE
A CAT LADY'S
OPIUM NAP

PUFFIN CLASSICS

Lewis Carroll, *Alice's Adventures in Wonderland*

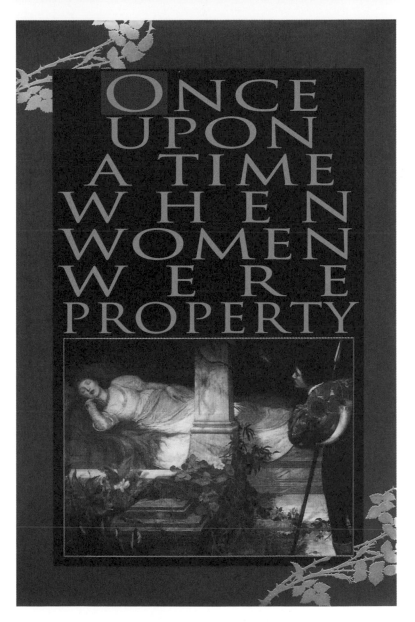

ONCE
UPON
A TIME
WHEN
WOMEN
WERE
PROPERTY

Jacob and Wilhelm Grimm, *Grimm's Fairy Tales*

Maurice Sendak, *Where the Wild Things Are*
Submitted by John Molina

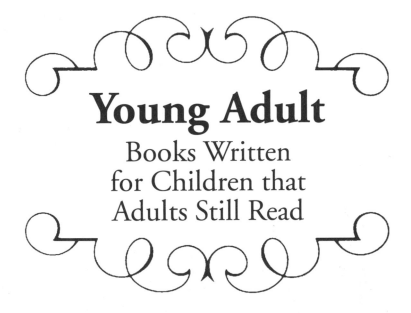

Young Adult

Books Written
for Children that
Adults Still Read

Judy Blume, *Are You There God? It's Me, Margaret*
Submitted by Anya Garrett

TEEN SEX IS OK IF ONE OF THEM HAS CANCER

NICHOLAS SPARKS

Nicholas Sparks, *A Walk to Remember*

Wilson Rawls, *Where the Red Fern Grows*

J. K. Rowling, *Harry Potter and the Goblet of Fire*
Submitted by John Molina

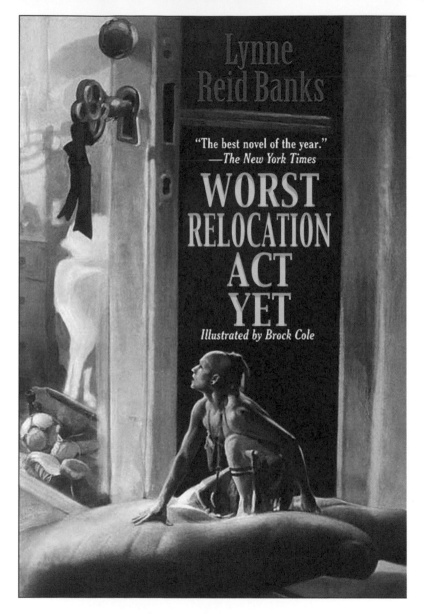

Lynne Reid Banks, *The Indian in the Cupboard*

the 107-year-old virgin

STEPHENIE MEYER

AUTHOR OF THE #1 BESTSELLING *TWILIGHT*, *NEW MOON*, AND *ECLIPSE*

Stephenie Meyer, *Breaking Dawn* (*Twilight Saga, Book 4*)
Submitted by Liz Holt

Ellen Raskin, *The Westing Game*

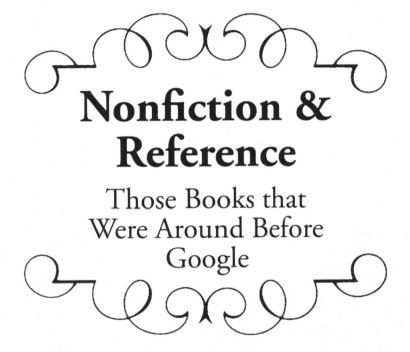

Nonfiction & Reference

Those Books that
Were Around Before
Google

The Merriam-Webster Dictionary

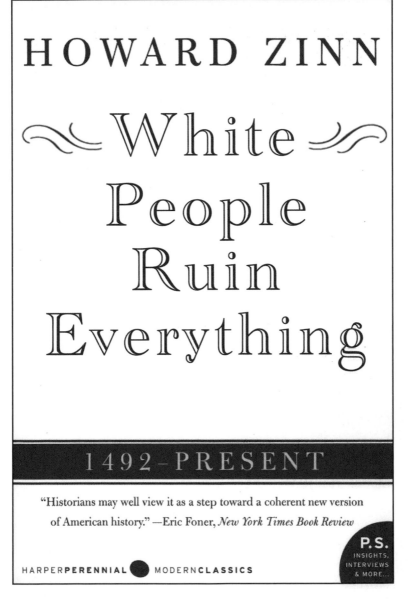

HOWARD ZINN

~ White ~
People
Ruin
Everything

1492–PRESENT

"Historians may well view it as a step toward a coherent new version
of American history." —Eric Foner, *New York Times Book Review*

HARPER**PERENNIAL** ● MODERN**CLASSICS**

P.S.
INSIGHTS,
INTERVIEWS
& MORE...

Howard Zinn, *A People's History of the United States*

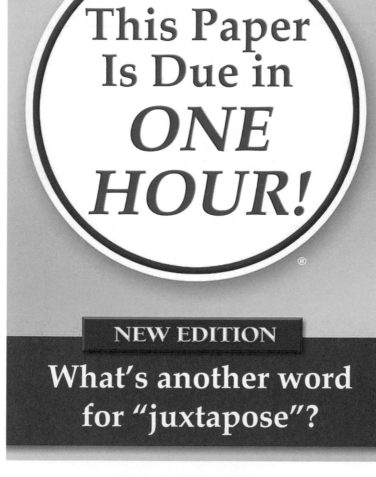

FIND THE RIGHT WORD FAST!

This Paper Is Due in *ONE HOUR!*

NEW EDITION

What's another word for "juxtapose"?

The Merriam-Webster Thesaurus

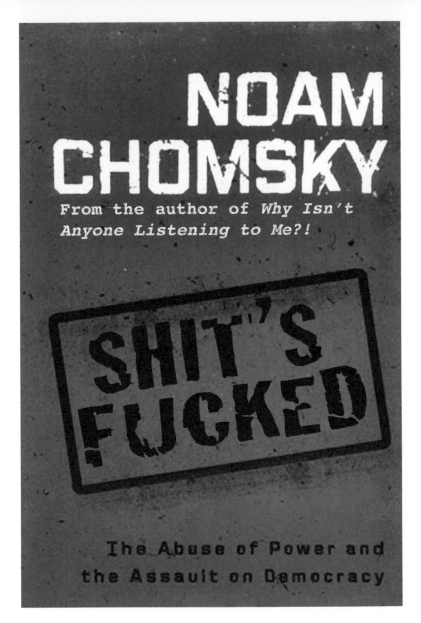

Noam Chomsky, *Failed States*

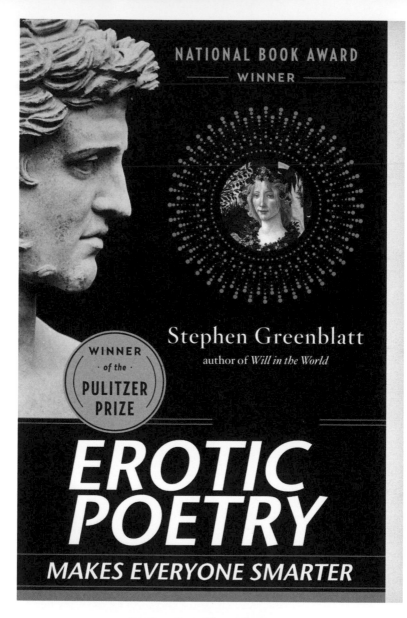

NATIONAL BOOK AWARD
— WINNER —

Stephen Greenblatt
author of *Will in the World*

WINNER
· of the ·
PULITZER
PRIZE

EROTIC POETRY

MAKES EVERYONE SMARTER

Stephen Greenblatt, *The Swerve*

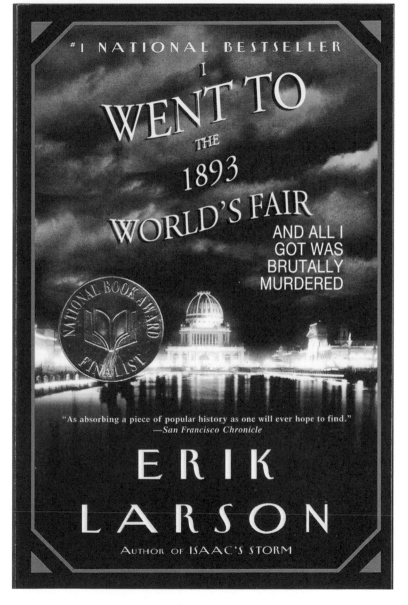

Erik Larson, *The Devil in the White City*
Submitted by Django Haskins

The #1 Bestselling Pregnancy Book
4TH EDITION

OVER 17 MILLION COPIES SOLD!

THERE WILL BE BLOOD

COMPLETELY NEW & REVISED

The pregnancy guide that reassuringly answers the questions of mothers- and fathers-to-be, from the planning stage through postpartum. Featuring a week-by-week look at the growth of your baby and complete chapters on pregnancy lifestyle, preconception, carrying twins—and more.

❖❖❖❖❖❖❖❖❖❖❖❖❖❖❖❖❖❖❖❖❖❖❖❖❖❖❖

By Heidi Murkoff
and Sharon Mazel

Foreword by Charles J. Lockwood, MD, Chair, Department of Obstetrics, Gynecology, and Reproductive Sciences, Yale University School of Medicine

Heidi Murkoff, *What to Expect When You're Expecting*
Submitted by Michael Molina

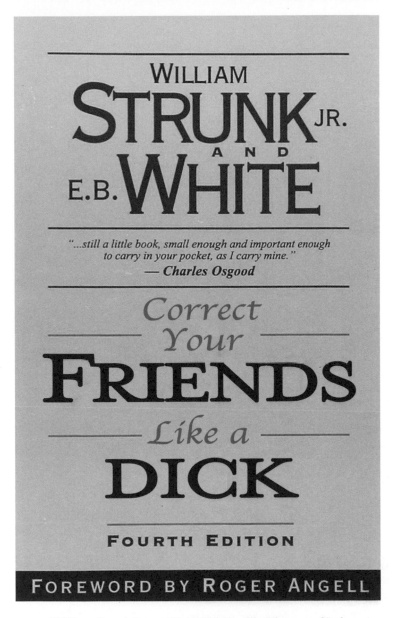

WILLIAM

STRUNK JR.

A N D

E.B. **WHITE**

*"...still a little book, small enough and important enough
to carry in your pocket, as I carry mine."*
— **Charles Osgood**

*Correct
Your*

FRIENDS

Like a

DICK

FOURTH EDITION

FOREWORD BY ROGER ANGELL

William Strunk Jr. and E. B. White, *The Elements of Style*
Submitted by Mike Lacher

59

OF COURSE I'VE READ THIS

IT WAS JUST A *LONG* TIME AGO

JARED DIAMOND

WITH A NEW AFTERWORD ABOUT THE MODERN WORLD

Jared Diamond, *Guns, Germs, and Steel*

Theater

Books that Are
Objectively Better if
Paid Actors Read
Them to You

EURIPIDES
HOW TO LOSE A GUY IN ONE DAY

A NEW TRANSLATION BY

ROBIN ROBERTSON

Euripides, *Medea*

WORST FACULTY KEY PARTY OF THE YEAR?

"Towers over the common run
of contemporary plays."
—*The New York Times*

EDWARD ALBEE

SIGNET

Edward Albee, *Who's Afraid of Virginia Woolf?*

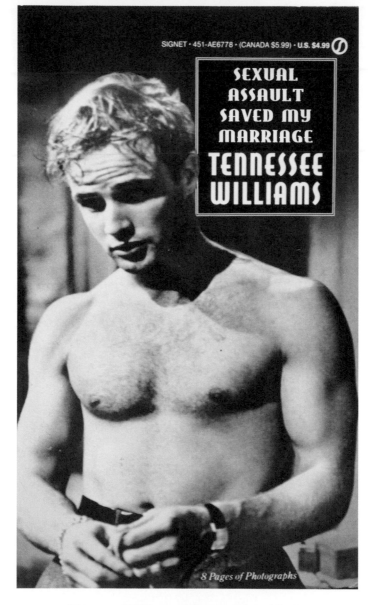

SIGNET · 451-AE6778 · (CANADA $5.99) · U.S. $4.99

SEXUAL ASSAULT SAVED MY MARRIAGE

TENNESSEE WILLIAMS

8 Pages of Photographs

Tennessee Williams, *A Streetcar Named Desire*

CATFISH

EDMOND ROSTAND

Includes detailed explanatory notes,
an overview of key themes, and more

Edmond Rostand, *Cyrano de Bergerac*

ENRICHED
CLASSIC

HOW I MET YOUR MOTHER

SOPHOCLES

Includes detailed explanatory notes,
an overview of key themes, and more

Sophocles, *Oedipus the King*
Submitted by Cassie Beh

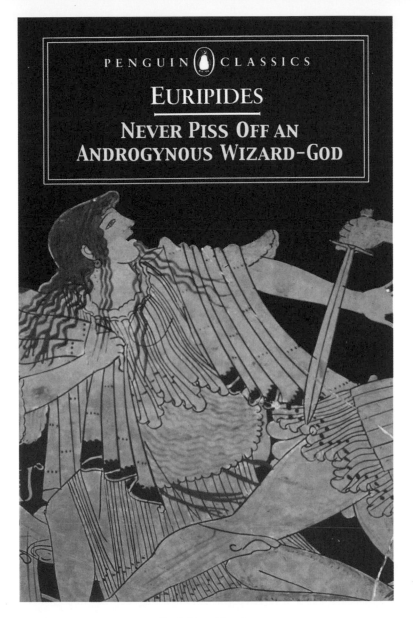

PENGUIN CLASSICS

EURIPIDES

NEVER PISS OFF AN
ANDROGYNOUS WIZARD-GOD

Euripides, *Bacchae*

**NEVER LISTEN
TO YOUR WIFE**

Edited by

Stephen Orgel

THE PELICAN
SHAKESPEARE

William Shakespeare, *Macbeth*

NEVER FAKE IT WITH
YOUR HUSBAND

Edited by
Peter Holland

THE PELICAN
SHAKESPEARE

William Shakespeare, *Romeo and Juliet*

INTERRACIAL MARRIAGE WILL KILL YOU

Edited by

Russ McDonald

THE PELICAN
SHAKESPEARE

William Shakespeare, *Othello*

CROSS-DRESSING HELPS
EVERYONE FIND LOVE

Edited by

Frances E. Dolan

THE PELICAN

SHAKESPEARE

William Shakespeare, *As You Like It*

GHOST DAD

Edited by

A. R. Braunmuller

THE PELICAN
SHAKESPEARE

William Shakespeare, *Hamlet*

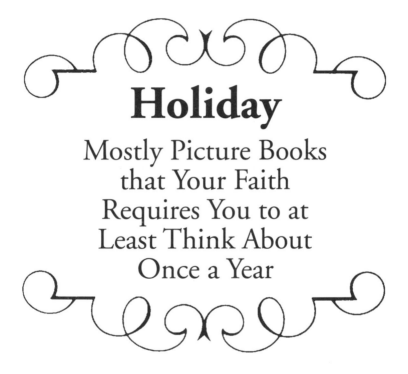

Holiday

Mostly Picture Books
that Your Faith
Requires You to at
Least Think About
Once a Year

DON'T STOP BELIEVIN'

Chris Van Allsburg, *The Polar Express*

Clement Moore and Jan Brett, *The Night Before Christmas*

Don't Get Too Close to
Your Friends or the Sun
Will Kill Them

Raymond Briggs

THE ORIGINAL CLASSIC STORY
WITH A NEW INTRODUCTION BY THE AUTHOR

Raymond Briggs, *The Snowman*

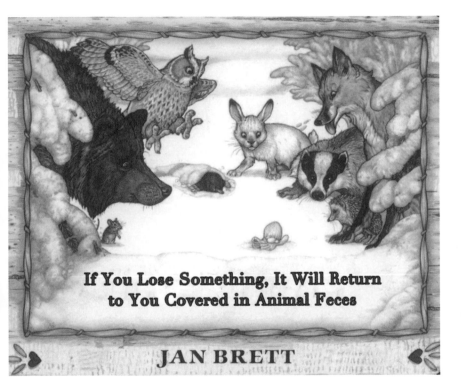

If You Lose Something, It Will Return
to You Covered in Animal Feces

JAN BRETT

Jan Brett, *The Mitten*

PEOPLE COMMEND A SHITTY GUY FOR BECOMING LESS SHITTY!

BY Dr. Seuss

Dr. Seuss, *How The Grinch Stole Christmas!*

RICH PEOPLE DESERVE SECOND CHANCES

CHARLES DICKENS

Charles Dickens, *A Christmas Carol*

Summer Reading

Books You Read
the Day Before the
Test at School

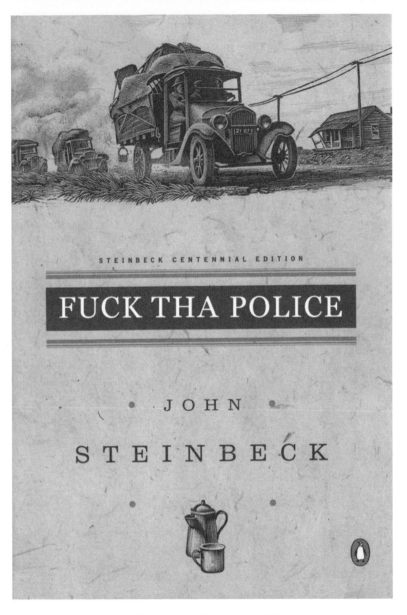

STEINBECK CENTENNIAL EDITION

FUCK THA POLICE

· JOHN ·

STEINBECK

John Steinbeck, *The Grapes of Wrath*

VLADIMIR NABOKOV

"The only convincing
love story of our century."
– *Vanity Fair*

Likable Rapists

Vladimir Nabokov, *Lolita*

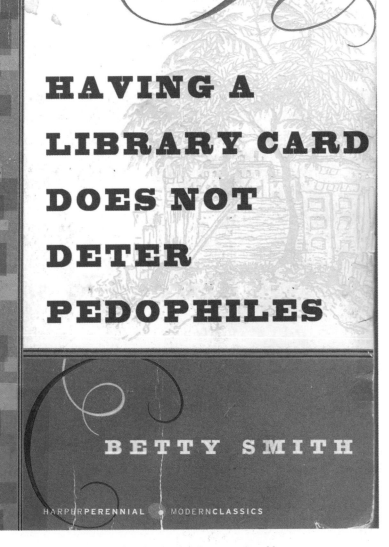

HAVING A LIBRARY CARD DOES NOT DETER PEDOPHILES

BETTY SMITH

HARPERPERENNIAL • MODERNCLASSICS

Betty Smith, *A Tree Grows in Brooklyn*

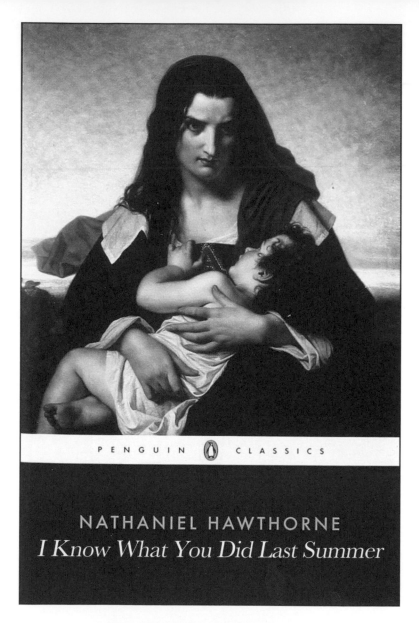

PENGUIN CLASSICS

NATHANIEL HAWTHORNE
I Know What You Did Last Summer

Nathaniel Hawthorne, *The Scarlet Letter*
Submitted by Megan Weiskopf

Ernest Hemingway, *The Sun Also Rises*
Submitted by Gabriel Laks

SYLVIA PLATH

INTERNSHIPS SUCK

HARPERPERENNIAL MODERNCLASSICS

Sylvia Plath, *The Bell Jar*

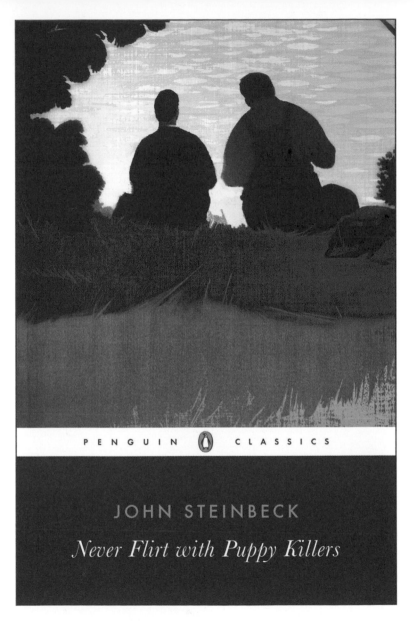

PENGUIN CLASSICS

JOHN STEINBECK

Never Flirt with Puppy Killers

John Steinbeck, *Of Mice and Men*

George Orwell, *Animal Farm*
Submitted by Tyler Snodgrass

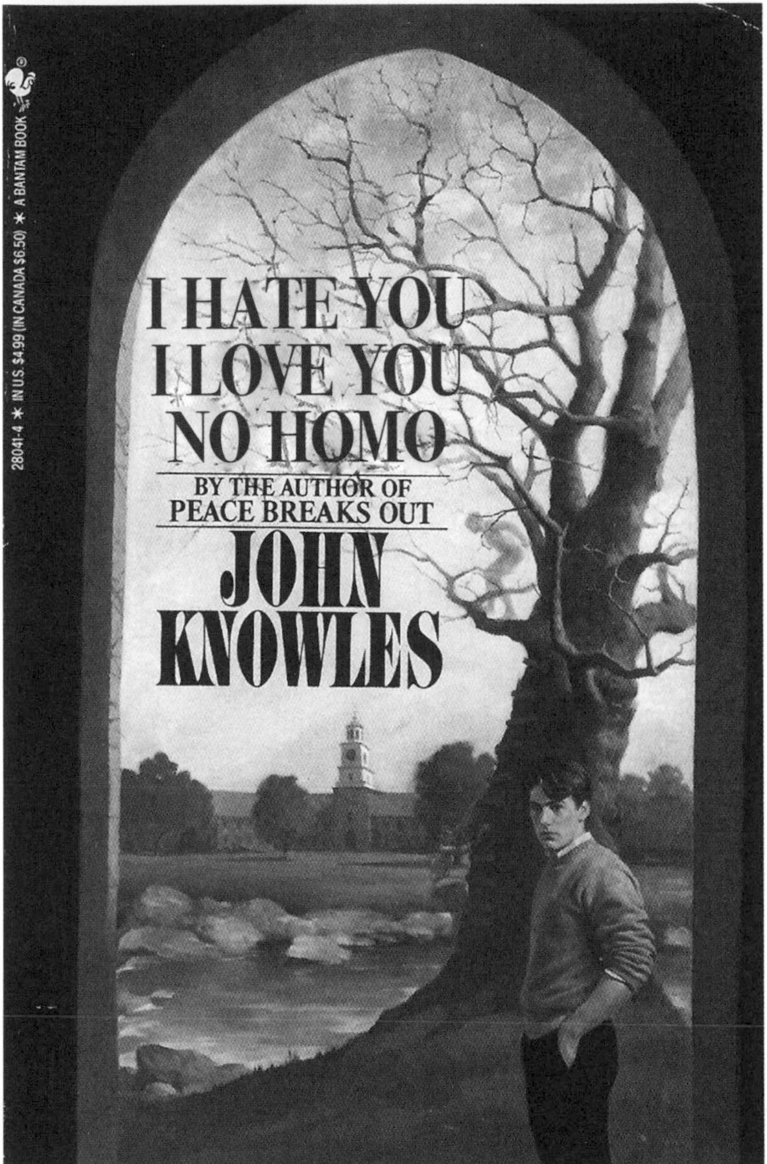
28041-4 ★ IN U.S. $4.99 (IN CANADA $6.50) ★ A BANTAM BOOK
I HATE YOU
I LOVE YOU
NO HOMO
BY THE AUTHOR OF
PEACE BREAKS OUT
JOHN
KNOWLES

John Knowles, *A Separate Peace*

AYN RAND
HATE-FUCKING & ARCHITECTURE
WITH AN INTRODUCTION BY THE AUTHOR

CENTENNIAL
EDITION

Ayn Rand, *The Fountainhead*
Submitted by Anya Garrett

Anthony Burgess, *A Clockwork Orange*

A WALK TO REMEMBER

J·R·R· TOLKIEN

THE LORD OF THE RINGS

J. R. R. Tolkien, *The Lord of the Rings* Trilogy
Submitted by Megan Pallante

Contemporary Fiction

Those Books People
Talk About at Parties that
"You've Definitely Heard of"
but Never Bothered
to Pick Up

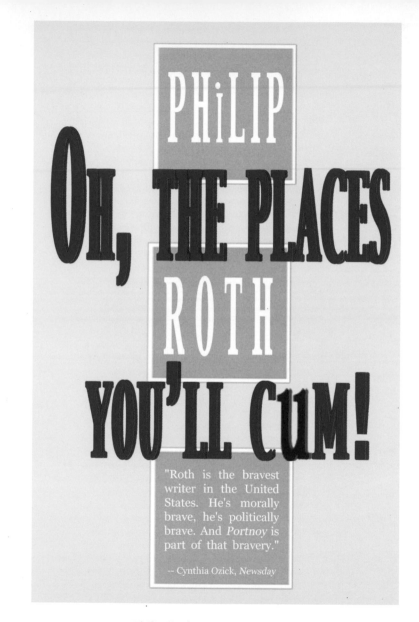

PHiLIP

OH, THE PLACES

ROTH

YOU'LL CUM!

"Roth is the bravest writer in the United States. He's morally brave, he's politically brave. And *Portnoy* is part of that bravery."

-- Cynthia Ozick, *Newsday*

Philip Roth, *Portnoy's Complaint*

GILLIAN

FLYNN

A TALE OF TWO
SHITTY PEOPLE

A NOVEL

Gillian Flynn, *Gone Girl*

From the author of *The Days of Abandonment*

It's Easier to Be Stabbed in Italy
Than Be Friends with Someone

"Elena Ferrante will blow you away."
—Alice Sebold, author of *The Lovely Bones*

Europa
editions

Elena Ferrante, *My Brilliant Friend*

"KIDNAPPER" IS THE ONLY GOOD JOB IN NORTH KOREA

A Novel

ADAM JOHNSON

Adam Johnson, *The Orphan Master's Son*

Everyone
Poops
a novel

K A T H R Y N
S T O C K E T T

Kathryn Stockett, *The Help*
Submitted by Mike Fath

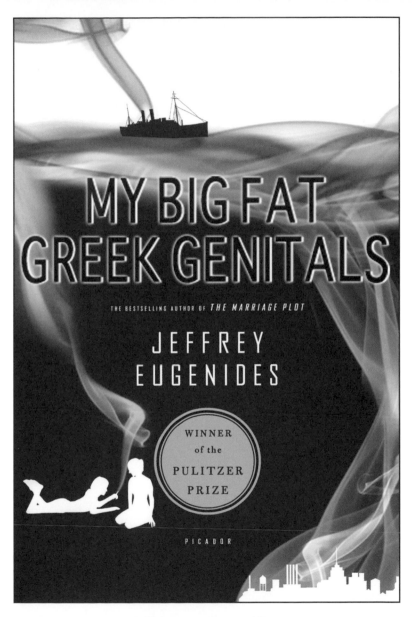

MY BIG FAT
GREEK GENITALS

THE BESTSELLING AUTHOR OF *THE MARRIAGE PLOT*

JEFFREY
EUGENIDES

WINNER of the
PULITZER
PRIZE

PICADOR

Jeffrey Eugenides, *Middlesex*
Submitted by Zack Ruskin

My Husband
Has Not Had
Sex with Me
Since 1998

E L James

#1 *New York Times* Bestseller

E. L. James, *Fifty Shades of Grey*

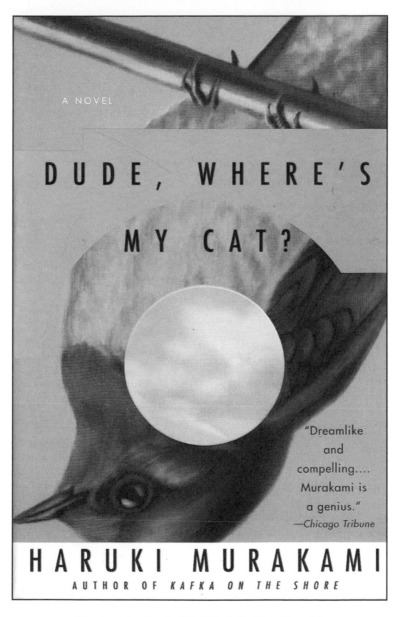

A NOVEL

DUDE, WHERE'S MY CAT?

"Dreamlike
and
compelling....
Murakami is
a genius."
—*Chicago Tribune*

HARUKI MURAKAMI

AUTHOR OF *KAFKA ON THE SHORE*

Haruki Murakami, *The Wind-Up Bird Chronicle*
Submitted by Michael Molina

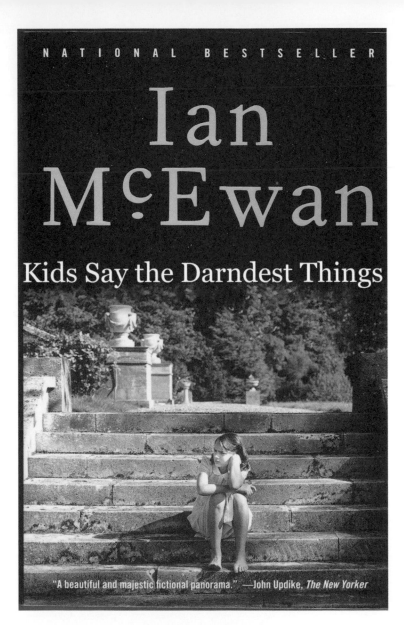

Ian McEwan

Kids Say the Darndest Things

"A beautiful and majestic fictional panorama." —John Updike, *The New Yorker*

Ian McEwan, *Atonement*
Submitted by Emily Grace Kane

HEAVEN

IS NOT
AS FUN AS
GHOST SEX

A novel

ALICE SEBOLD

Alice Sebold, *The Lovely Bones*

DONNA TARTT

AUTHOR OF *THE LITTLE FRIEND*

STUDYING

CLASSICS GIVES PEOPLE AN INSATIABLE THIRST FOR HUMAN BLOOD

A NOVEL

"Enthralling. . . . A remarkably powerful novel [and] a ferociously well-paced entertainment. . . . Forceful, cerebral, and impeccably controlled."
—*The New York Times*

Donna Tartt, *The Secret History*

Neal Stephenson, *Snow Crash*

THIS
IS THE
FIRST
BOOK I'VE
READ IN
SIX YEARS
STIEG
LARSSON

A NOVEL

Stieg Larsson, *The Girl with the Dragon Tattoo*

Acknowledgments

Thank you to Anya Garrett who helped me put this book together, taught me Photoshop, and kept me sane for the past six years. That's the hardest work anyone's done for this book, really. I love you.

Thank you to everyone who contributed to the site, and everyone named in this book for submitting titles! You're all better at retitling than I am.

Thanks also to Community Bookstore, Housing Works Bookstore Cafe, and Marcus Parks for producing my podcast about books for so long. Thank you to the staff at Someecards for putting up with my opinions on comedy and books.

Other books by Dan Wilbur

How Not to Read: Harnessing the Power of a Literature-Free Life

Andrews McMeel Publishing
a division of Andrews McMeel Universal
1130 Walnut Street, Kansas City, Missouri 64106

www.andrewsmcmeel.com

16 17 18 19 20 SDB 10 9 8 7 6 5 4 3 2 1

ISBN: 978-1-4494-7806-3

Library of Congress Control Number: 2015956408

Editor: Patty Rice
Art Director: Tim Lynch
Production Manager: Tamara Haus
Production Editor: Erika Kuster